and then it's spring

Julie Fogliano

ILLUSTRATED BY

Erin E. Stead

A NEAL PORTER BOOK
ROARING BROOK PRESS
NEW YORK

First you have brown,
all around you have brown

then there are seeds

and a wish for rain,

and then it rains

and it is still brown,
but a hopeful, very possible sort of brown,

an *is that a little green?*

no, it's just brown sort of brown

then it is a week

and you worry
about those little seeds

and if maybe it was the birds,

or maybe it was the bears and all that stomping,
because bears can't read signs
that say things like
"please do not stomp here—
there are seeds
and they are trying"

and then it is one more week,

and the brown,
still brown,
has a greenish hum
that you can only hear
if you put your ear to the ground
and close your eyes

and then it is one more week

and a sunny day,
that sunny day that happens
right after that rainy day

and you walk outside
to check on all that brown,

but the brown isn't around
and now you have green,
all around
you have
green.

for enzo, nico, and josh,
who love to go outside and notice things
—j.f.

for julie, josh, george, jason,
jennifer, nick, patty, and sara
—e.s.

Text copyright © 2012 by Julie Fogliano
Illustrations copyright © 2012 by Erin E. Stead
A Neal Porter Book
Published by Roaring Brook Press
Roaring Brook Press is a division of Holtzbrinck Publishing Holdings Limited Partnership
175 Fifth Avenue, New York, New York 10010
mackids.com

Library of Congress Cataloging-in-Publication Data
Fogliano, Julie.
And then it's spring / Julie Fogliano ; illustrated by Erin E. Stead. —
1st ed.
    p. cm.
"A Neal Porter Book."
Summary: Simple text reveals the anticipation of a boy who, having planted
seeds while everything around is brown, fears that something has gone wrong
until, at last, the world turns green.
ISBN: 978-1-59643-624-4
[1. Spring—Fiction. 2. Gardens—Fiction.] I. Stead, Erin E., ill. II. Title. III. Title:
And then it is spring.
PZ7.F6763And 2012
[E]—dc22

2010049379

Roaring Brook Press books are available for special promotions and premiums.
For details contact: Director of Special Markets, Holtzbrinck Publishers.

First edition 2012
Book design by Philip C. Stead and Jennifer Browne
Printed in China by Toppan Leefung Printing Ltd., Dongguan City, Guangdong Province

1 3 5 7 9 10 8 6 4 2